no two alike

ISBN 978-0-545-52208-3

Copyright © 2011 by Keith Baker. All rights reserved.
Published by Scholastic Inc., 557 Broadway, New York,
NY 10012, by arrangement with Simon & Schuster
Books for Young Readers, an imprint of Simon &
Schuster Children's Publishing Division. SCHOLASTIC
and associated logos are trademarks and/or registered
trademarks of Scholastic Inc.

12 11 10 9 8 7   13 14 15 16 17/0

Printed in the U.S.A.   40

First Scholastic printing, November 2012

Book design by Sonia Chaghatzbanian
The text for this book is set in ITC Benguiat.
The illustrations for this book are rendered digitally.

no two alike

Keith Baker

SCHOLASTIC INC.

No two snowflakes are alike,

almost, *almost* . . .

but not quite.

No two nests,
so soft and round,

no two tracks upon the ground.

No two branches, no two leaves,

no two forests, full of trees.

No two fences, long and low,

no two roads—where do they go?

No two bridges, wood or stone,

no two houses—
anyone home?

No two friends, large or small,
no two alike . . .

among you all!

Are we the same—

just alike?

Almost, *almost* . . .

but not quite.